LOOK UP!

Jung Jin-Ho

Holiday House / New York

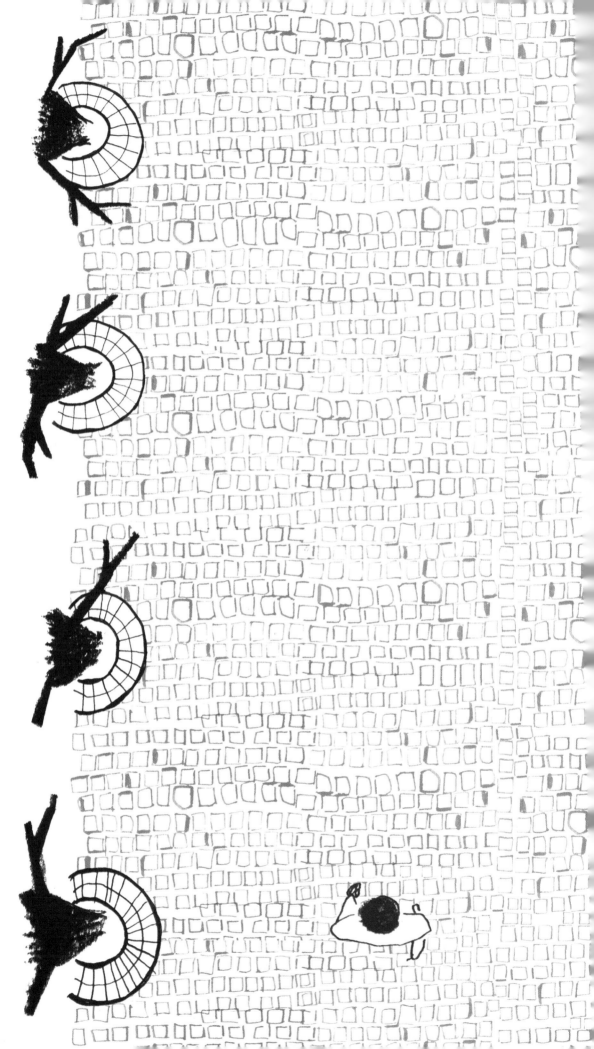

SLAM!

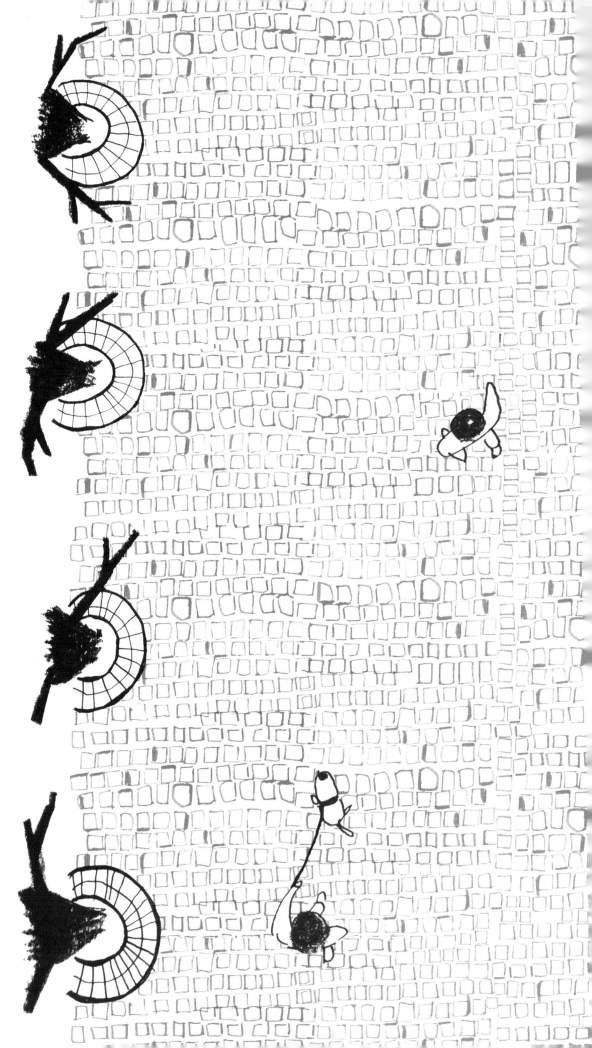

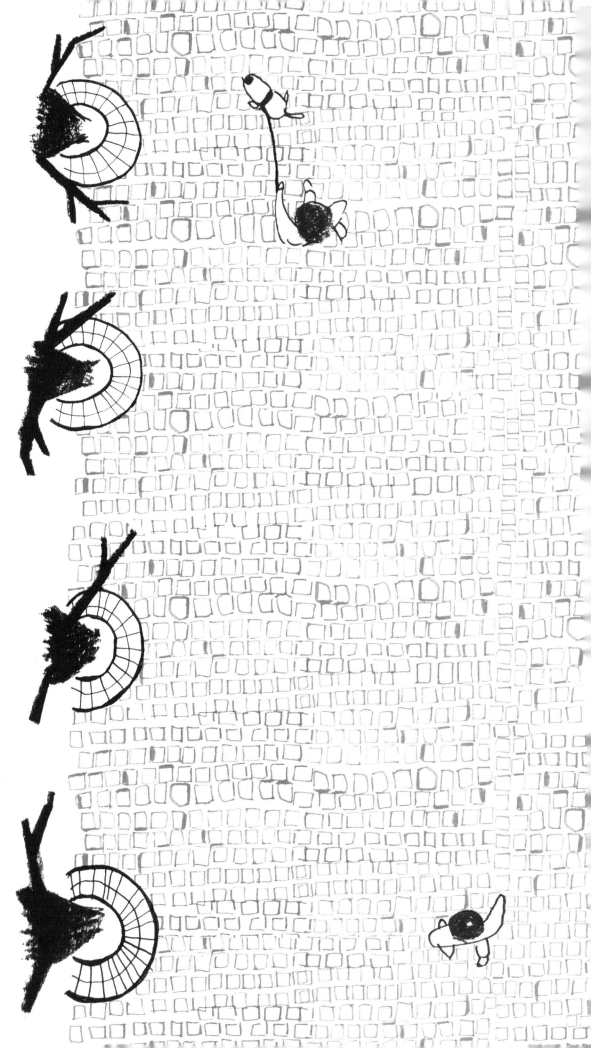

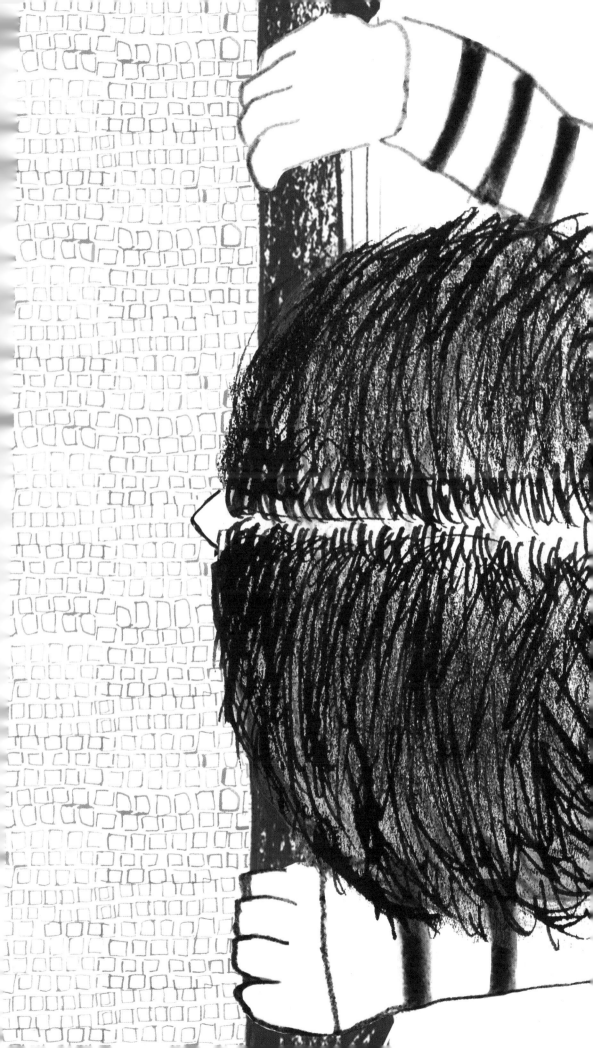

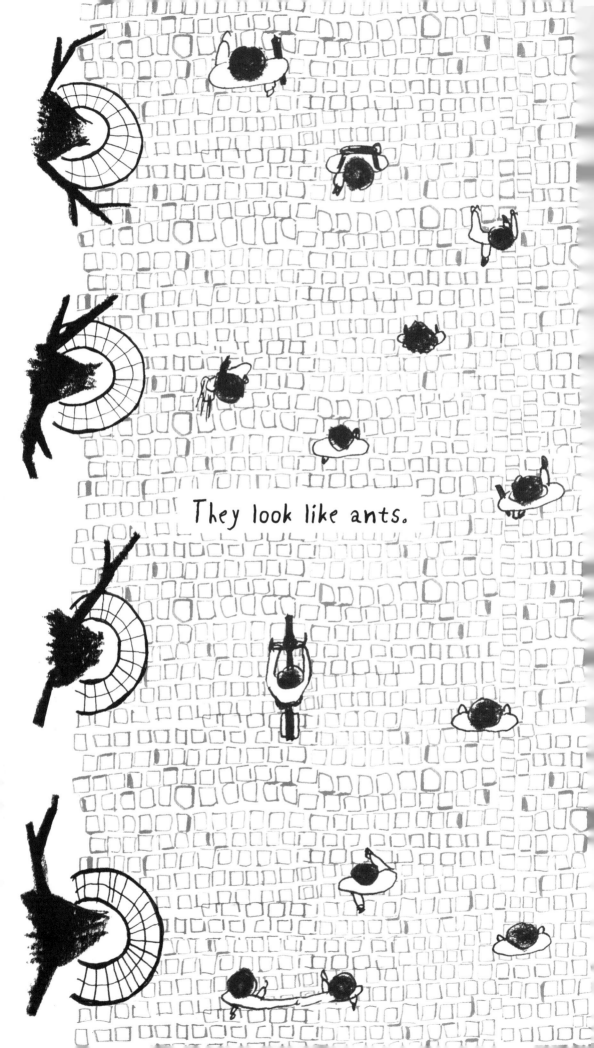

They look like ants.

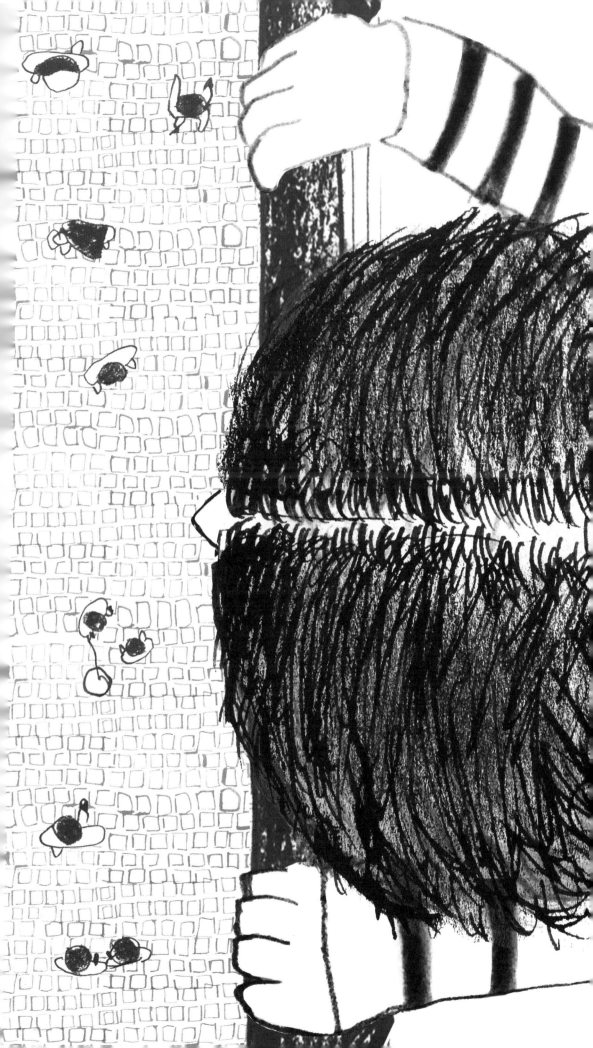

Look up!

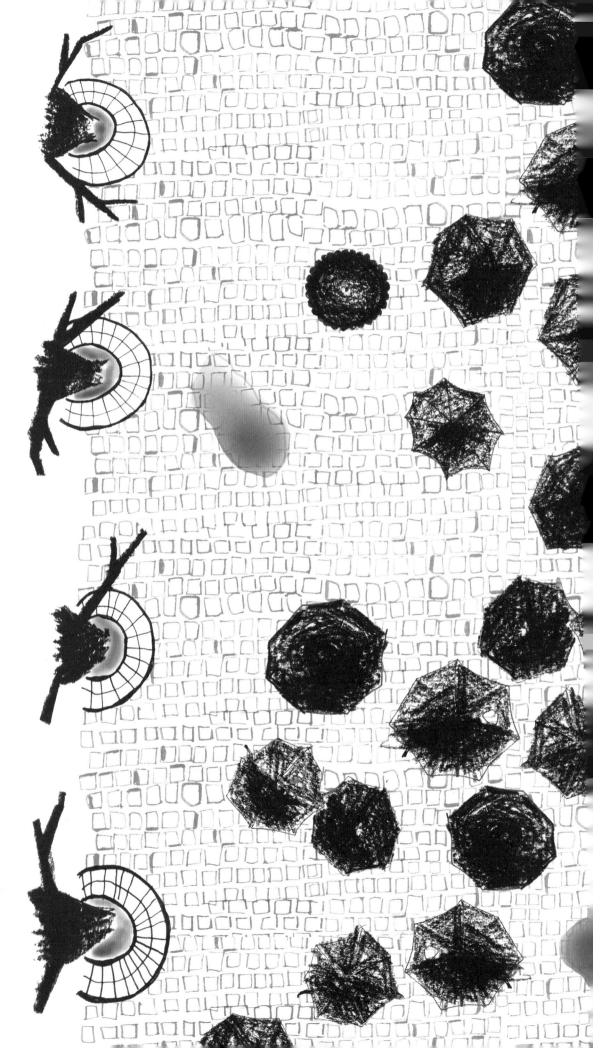

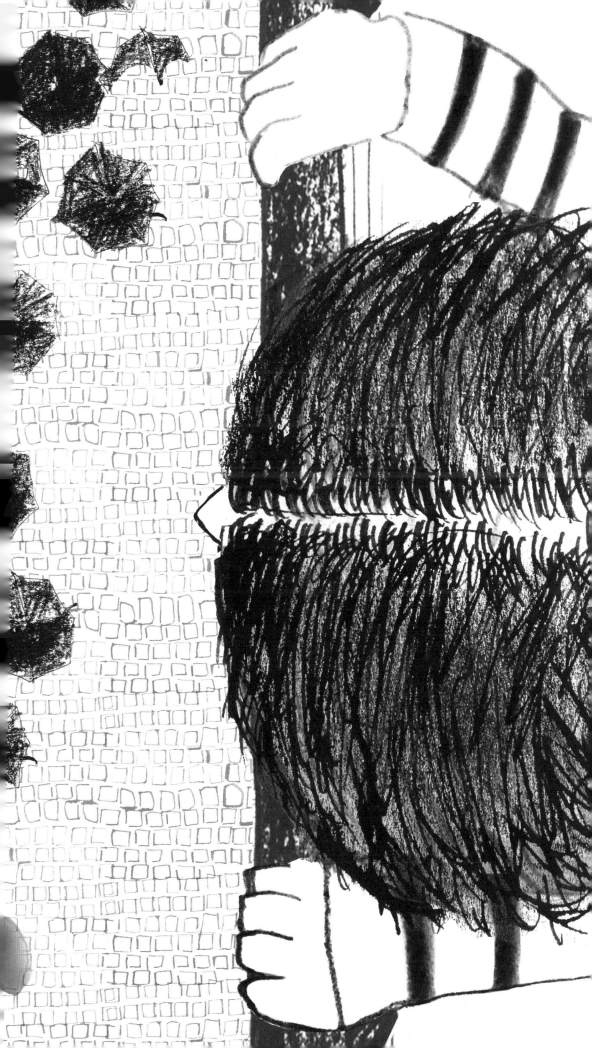

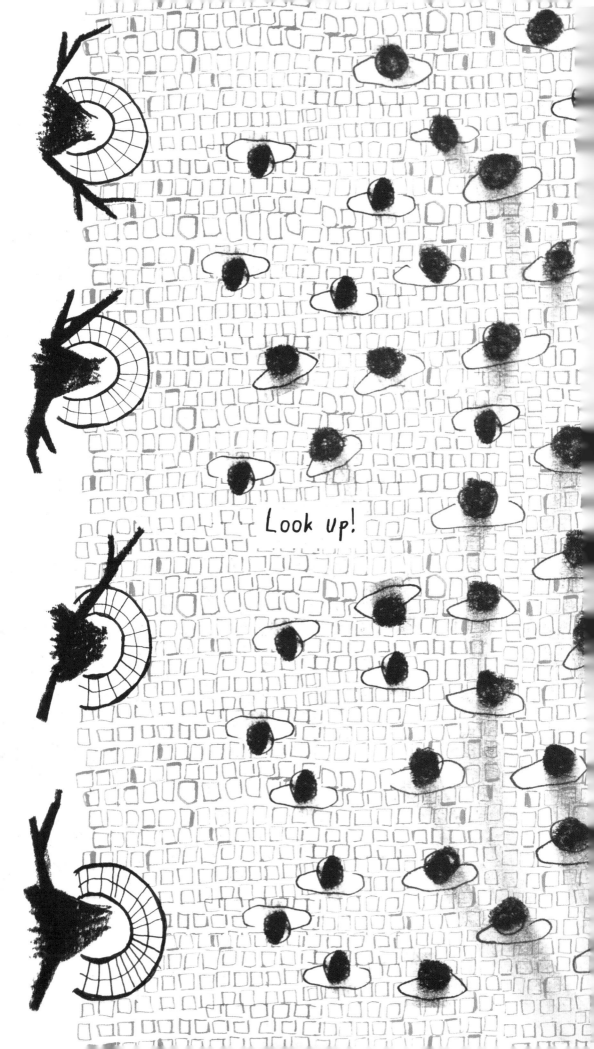

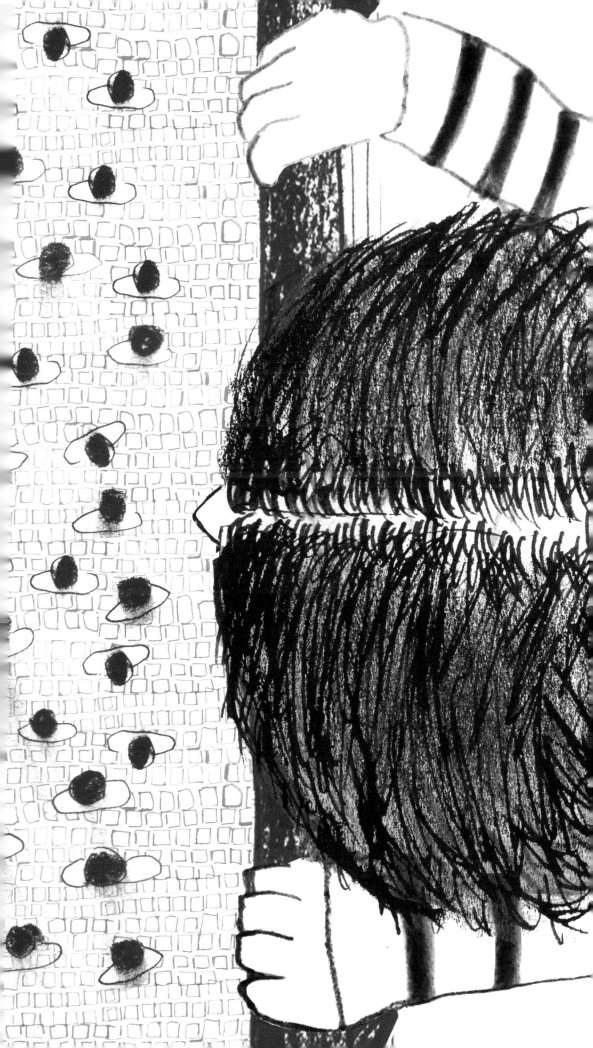

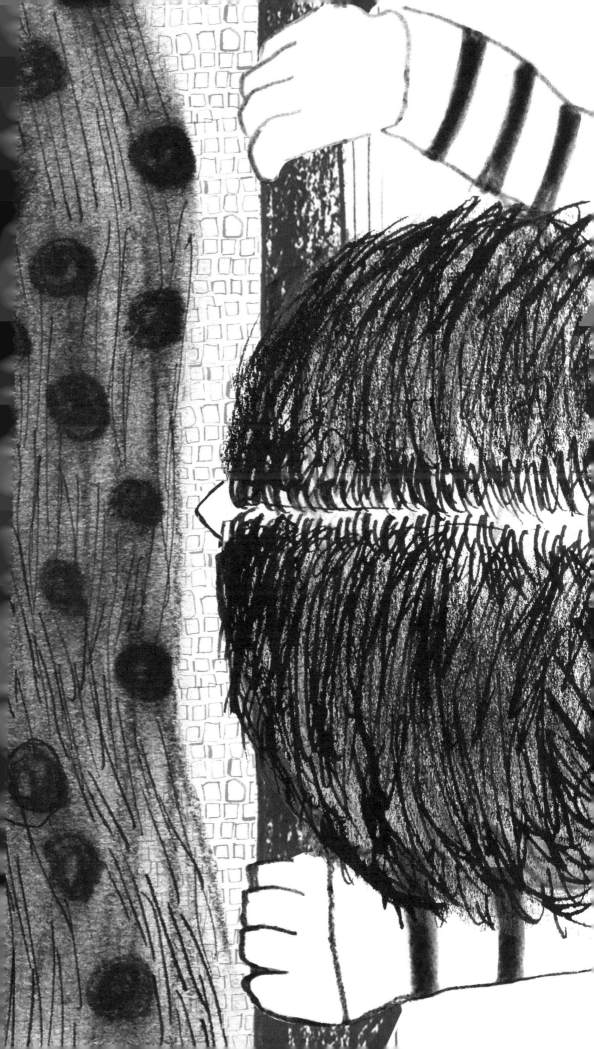

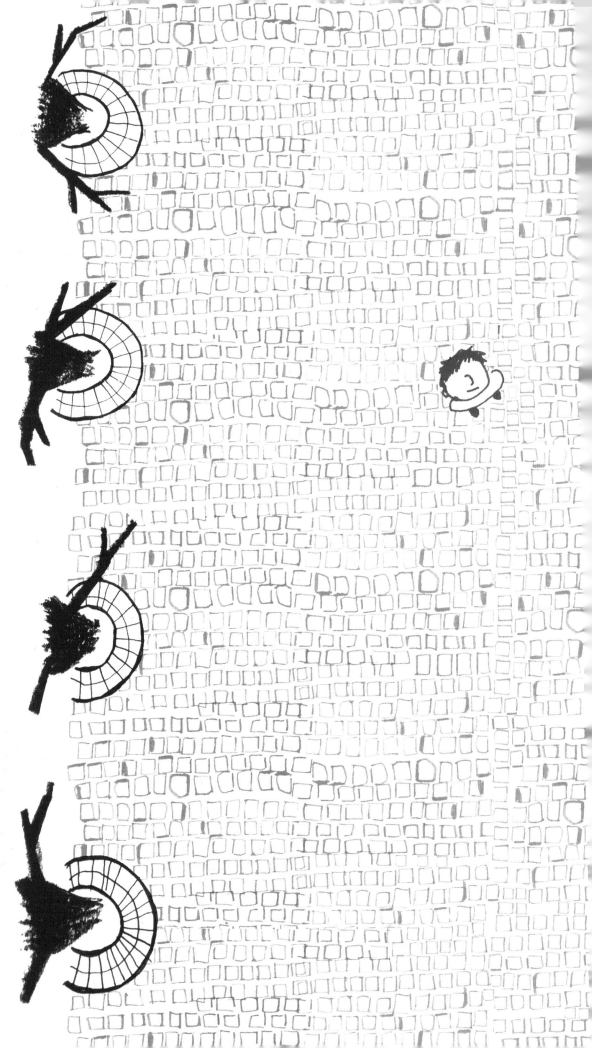

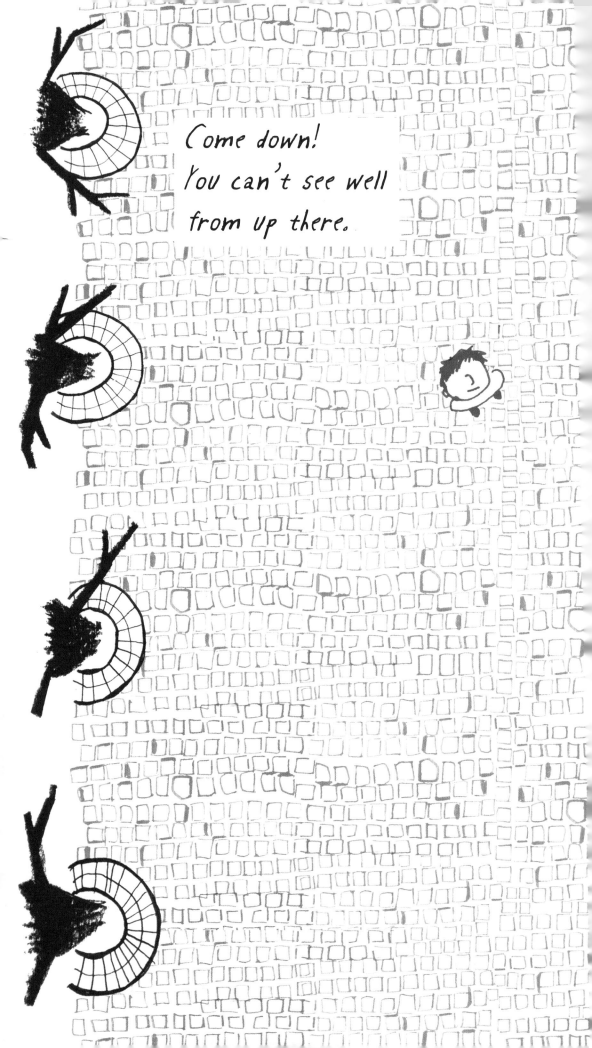

You're right!
I can only
see the tops
of people's
heads!

Why are you lying on the sidewalk?

So the girl up there can see me.

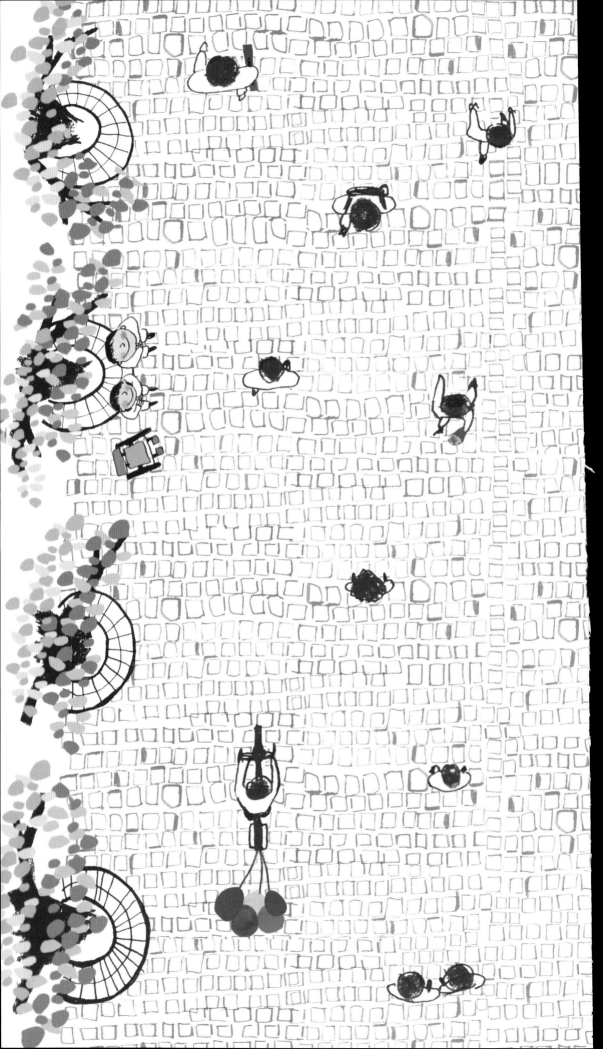

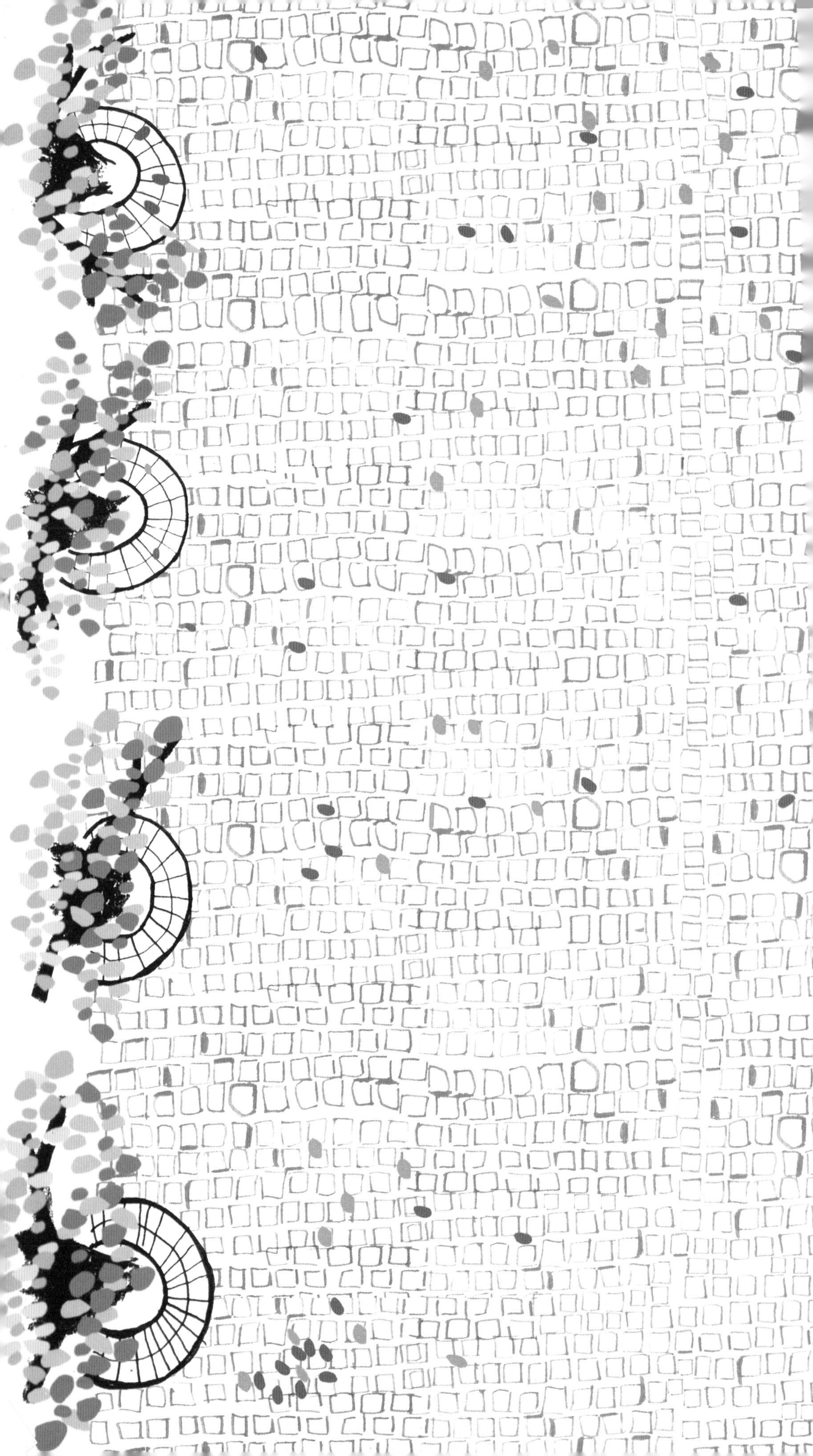